To all the Medical Fetish Fans,
those who have dreams of being a
doctors' patient,
and those who dream of having a
patient.

And to the doctors, and the
patients, out there,
who can make those dreams come
true.

The Visiting Surgeon
Book 4

<u>The Visiting Surgeon 4</u>

<u>Part 1</u>

Jade groaned, her stomach flat against her bed, her hands sliding under her pillow and gripping her head board. Moaning in her sleep. She was picturing him, her surgeon, following her, telling her she was going to be his. He had her pinned to the table before she could say anything or move. Her clothes gone as though she had never worn them. His cock was rock hard and he smiled at her, pinning her arms above her head, telling her he was going to take her, to make her his. Jade rolled in her bed, her hands grabbing another pillow on her bed and tossing it over the side as she struggled in her sleep. Her clit was tingling, she wanted him inside of her so badly. Wondering what it would feel like...but just as he started to slide his cock into her, Jade woke up...

She blinked looking around her room, but only saw blackness. During the night she had rolled over, covering her head with the blankets. Brushing her face against her satin pillow case, her hips bucked against her bed. Her vaginal core felt so empty, her clit felt cheated. Groaning in frustration her hands gripped the sides of her pillow. She hadn't had many, if any, wet dreams in her life, but this one...oooh how she wished the dream had continued on. She needed to feel him inside of her. She needed him to ease the throbbing in her pussy and the pulsing in her clit. Moaning, she took a breath, the scent of her arousal trapped within the blankets on her bed and filling her own lungs. Pressing her hips against her bed she lifted her head up and moved it side to side, freeing herself from the blankets. Blinking at the light she looked at the wall to her side and sighed. "Thank gawd he wasn't here to know!" But what if he had been? Would he have finished the dream? Rolled her over? Pin her hands above her head, and thrust his cock deep and hard into her? Or would he watch her press into her bed, gripping her pillow, wishing he was between her legs. The more she thought about it, the more she felt her panties getting wet. Forcing herself to kick off the blankets and roll onto her side.

Sighing, she convinced herself to get up and strip off her pyjamas. Her shirt collar had a bit of sweat on it, from tossing and turning in the bed, dreaming of passionate sex with a surgeon. She laughed at herself as she tossed the shirt into her laundry bin. Moving to the bathroom she grabbed a towel and put it by the shower. Stepping back to her room she undid the string on her pyjama bottoms and shimmied them off her hips. As she bent down to take them off she caught the scent of her arousal again. Damn. "That was one hell of a dream." She chuckled then turned on the water in the shower. Testing that the water was fairly warm, she slowly took her panties off, imagining Doctor Tyler standing there watching her. Taking one side of the satin material, sliding it off her hip, then the other. As she pulled them down and let them fall to the floor, she smiled. Would he be turned on? Would he press her up against the bathroom wall, trapping her with his body? Would he force her legs open with his knee and let his free hand slide between her legs, feeling her wetness? Or would he bend her over her bathroom sink, spanking her bare ass until it was a light shade of red, before his hand 'accidentally' moved lower, his fingers slipping into her, wiggling deeper; teasing her hungry vagina while he continued to spank her. Hmm maybe he would do both, before forcing her back onto his table, in front of all the doctors.

Jade groaned, picking up her panties. She still couldn't believe that all those doctors would be her professors, or others in the industry that she would meet soon. How could he force her to be so open and at all of their mercy?

Crumpling her satin panties into a ball she reached out from the bathroom door and tossed them into the laundry bin, then stepped into the shower. The water felt good moving over her skin, taking the soap with it, even between her legs. Oh how she wanted to touch herself, how she really wanted him to touch her. But she was going to be late, she was probably already late, but she couldn't risk one of her professors getting a hold of the hot masked surgeon and letting him know she had missed a class. Turning off the shower, she picked up the towel and dried herself off. The material, though soft, made her clit tingle as she brought it over her lower abdomen. She imagined his bare hand moving side to side across her stomach, moving lower and lower, until his fingers just touched her clit....Jade tossed the towel aside and moved into the bedroom. She had to stop thinking about him. Had to stop thinking about the dream!

Glancing at the clock she gasped and made a face. Between the dream and her shower, she was already over 2 hours late for class. Holding her bra in her right hand she shrugged. If she was already that late, she might as well masturbate before going to class. It would be easier than trying to sit in class, crossing and uncrossing her legs, hoping that the seam of her pants brushed her clit to ease some of the heat between her legs.

Lying down on her bed, looking up at the ceiling, she spread her legs, using one hand to spread her vaginal lips, while the other started to slowly rub and even pinch her clit. Moaning, she closed her eyes, her hips starting to move as she pictured him. His fingers spanking her for losing focus, but then rubbing the sting from her clit. Moving lower to her entrance, just poking inside of her as his lips wrapped around her clit. Jade started breathing faster, her clit swelling under her fingertips. "Hmmmmmmmm....ahhhhhhhhhh......"

Her head pressed back into the pillow as her body tensed, she was going to cum...

Something hit her face, she figured maybe it was a piece of her blanket falling back on her. Opening her eyes, and bringing the one hand up, that was parting her vaginal lips, so that she could still touch her clit, she took her panties off her face...the panties she had just thrown into the laundry bin...

Jades heart stopped, as did her fingers on her clit. But her body was so excited, her pussy so wet, her hips kept bucking, begging for attention. Her vaginal core, still feeling empty and cheated from the dream. Looking towards the laundry basket she saw Doctor Tyler standing there, his arms crossed, looking down at her. She bit her bottom lip, hoping it was a dream..

"Young lady!!!" He kept his voice stern and loud, though his cock was throbbing, aching at the site of her exposed and very aroused pussy. Her labia puffy, pink, and oh so very wet. "You have obviously not learned your lesson about losing your focus!"

Jade knew then it wasn't a dream. She was torn between asking him to touch her, to make her cum, or at the very least let her finish masturbating. She needed so badly to come. Her stomach was so tense, her clit throbbed, her slit was contracting, hoping to find a cock to draw deep inside of her.

"You are very late for your classes and when I come to find out why, I find you lying on your bed, legs spread, touching your very naughty clit!!!" Doctor Tyler walked up to her, placing his hands on her inner thighs, forcing her legs further apart. "What's worse, is your panties were soaking wet." He hoped she couldn't feel his hands trembling against her thighs, as he forced himself not to bury his cock inside of her. Quickly bringing one hand down, he gave her very sensitive and aroused clit 3 hard spanks. SPANK SPANK SPANK. She gasped, but her body arched up after the third, as though hoping he would touch her again. Putting his hands back on her thighs, forcing her to stay open he looked at her. "I think I will need to take some more drastic medical approaches to this dirty habit of yours, young lady." Doctor Tyler did his best to hide the grin on his face as he pictured thrusting his cock deep and hard into her. The glistening wetness on her lips now, covering his balls, and letting his cock glide easily into and out of her. His 'drastic medical approaches' were all about him driving her need to the edge...and perhaps his as well.

"Ohhh, oh please doctor! I'm...I'm sorry!" Jade chewed the inside of her cheek. What was he going to do? And why was the thought of him and his drastic medical approaches, making her wetter?

Doctor Tyler pinched her swollen clit, watching as it budded out further from the clitoral hood with the action. He resisted the urge to lick his lips. Taking his hand away he gave her clit another 3 hard spanks. SPANK. SPANK.

SPANK. "Stand up. I'm taking you downstairs."

Jades stomach fluttered and she moaned. His spankings had stung, but the stinging had now turned into an erotic burn, making her clit hot, begging for more attention. As she stood and looked at him, she needed him inside of her. She still felt so empty from her dream ending before...she swallowed...she was in enough trouble as it was, she couldn't think about the dream now...not while he was taking her...to...to be on his table...

<u>PART 2</u>

As Doctor Tyler left her bedroom Jade grabbed a large hoodie and quickly pulled it on over her head. Though it didn't cover all of her, it covered enough. If anyone saw them walking down the hall way they would just think she had shorts on underneath it, though it would be stretching it, as the bottom of the hoodie came to just below her pubic area. As they walked out of her dorm she was glad he was too distracted to notice, otherwise he might have made her take it off for the walk.

Taking a couple quick steps to catch up Jade watched him from behind. He looked so good in scrubs, even from his back side. His shoulders strong, like she could lay against him, resting her head on them, listening to him breathe or even the sound of his own heart beat. His back and hips looked lean and toned, like he could push her up against the wall, pull out his cock and thrust it into her while he pinned her there. She moaned softly making Doctor Tyler stop. Jade held her breath but he didn't turn around. As he started walking again and down the stairs, she watched his ass. Hmmm his scrubs were perfect. She could make out his cheeks so easily. It would give her something to hold on to while he penetrated her and made her pant. Her fingers squeezing the bare cheeks into her palm. Maybe even giving him a few spanks in return to the ones he had given her. Would he moan if she did? Jade bit her tongue to keep from moaning herself as her hands pushed down on the front of her hoodie, trying hard not to rub her clit as she thought about him.

She could picture it, he would have her down on her back, after catching her masturbating in her bedroom. Hmm yes, his cock would be so hard and swollen after watching her rub her own clit. He would climb up onto the bed, forcing her legs apart, pinning her hands above her head as a warning. Then his cock would force her wide open, filling her in one swift thrust. Oh how she would gasp and likely scream at the surprise invasion. But she would be dripping wet, like she was now, he would slide so easily into her. The surprise would cause her to bring her hands down, cupping his ass as he leaned over her, his forearms on the bed beside her head, holding himself up. She would look up at him, her eyes looking into his, making her heart skip a beat and her clit tingle. She could feel her vaginal muscles gripping his rock hard cock, wanting more. She would squeeze his one ass cheek then spank his other. No doubt he would look at her, maybe give her his stern dominant, 'I'm in control,' surgeon look. She would be tempted to not spank him again, but her playful side would spank him any way. He would growl, but it would be low...Jade moaned as she thought about it, her hands twisting in the hoodie fabric...he would look at her then lean his head in and nip at her collar bone. Kissing her neck then biting her softly in the same spot, claiming her, while reprimanding her for spanking him...yet she would do it again. Jade closed her eyes and moaned running smack into Doctor Tyler.

"What the...?!" Jade gasped and looked down, Doctor Tyler was beneath her, her body on top of his, her breasts pressed against his chest, making her wish she hadn't been wearing a hoodie. She bit her bottom lip. "Get off me young lady!" But all she could picture was his mouth on her neck, his cock inside of her. Jade took a breath and leaned in, nipping at the base of his neck, her hips humping against the growing bulge in his scrub pants. His body was tense, his hands on her shoulders now slipping further down her waist. His intent to push her off of him changing. Slipping under her hoodie. Oh, he felt so good against her bare skin, his hands skilled as he knew where to go. Knew how hard to touch her. Letting her know that though she was on top of him, her pussy bucking into his cock, he was still her doctor, he was still in control. Sliding up, cupping her breasts. She moaned against his neck, her mouth sucking hard, she would leave a hickey but she didn't care. She moved her hands under his shoulders holding onto him, her hips pressing against his. He couldn't stand it either. Taking one hand off of her body he moved it between his legs freeing his cock. Groaning low she bit his neck as the tip of his cock touched her entrance. As she felt the head press against her, she moved her hips and pressed down, forcing his cock to....

Doctor Tyler snapped his fingers in front of her face. "Hey!!!" He watched as she stood in the middle of the hallway, just outside the door, her legs crossed, eyes closed. Her hands were twisted in the hoodie, gripping the material so tight her knuckles were turning white. Her bottom lip trapped between her teeth. She was breathing hard, moaning. He snapped his fingers again. "Hey!" His hand touched her shoulder and she jumped.

Jades' eyes shot open and went wide as she stared at him. Dear gawd it had all been a day dream. "I...I ...I..." She wanted to say something, anything, but all she could think about was his hand on her shoulder, and the incredible heat between her legs. She needed to cum.

"You what, young lady?!" Doctor Tyler felt his cock instantly jump. Even though she had a hoodie on and was covered up, he could tell she was about to cum. She looked so hot with her hands twisted in her hoodie, causing the material to ride up just a bit higher and expose her freshly shaved pubic mound. He moved his hand around her neck then pushed her up against the wall, feeling his own heart pound as her pulse brushed against his palm. The beat was fast, strong, erotic and gave away the arousal she was trying, but failing, too hide. Leaning in he looked directly into her eyes. "You were being naughty weren't you?...You lost focus didn't you?!"

Jade panted. If he hadn't pushed her against the

wall she wouldn't have been able to move. She would have been afraid to move. "I...I...I...." She wanted to move her eyes away from him but she couldn't, she was trapped. Trapped in his power. Trapped in his passion. Trapped in his control.

Doctor Tyler brought his hand to her legs, giving her pubic mound a little spank. "Spread. Your. Legs." He squeezed his hand a bit around her neck, keeping his tone strict, but he was so hot. His cock was throbbing. Catching her in the act, not once, but twice. Hmmm he could just image how hot she was inside right now. How tight her muscles would wrap around his cock. Jade moved against the wall, taking a couple slow steps, spreading her legs for him. He breathed in, her scent was so strong. It made his mouth water to taste her, his cock almost demand to answer the call of her arousal. Keeping his eyes on hers he could see her pupils were dilated. She was excited, she wanted him.

He took another breath, letting his hand slip between her thighs. He didn't even need to go past her clit, she was so wet his fingertips felt it instantly. Squeezing his hand around her neck to keep his focus on her, his hand slid further, cupping her entire pussy, the tips of his fingers just poking inside of her. "Bad girl!" He rubbed the heel of his hand against her clit. "I think your body, your pussy, needs a very through exam." She moaned, her hips slowly moving against his hand, wanting more. Doctor Tyler groaned and forced himself to take a step back from her. He pointed to the door. "Get your naughty ass inside that operating room now, young lady!!"

Jade moaned in frustration, but his tone was so strict she quickly moved off the wall and went to the doorway. Peeking out from behind the door frame, she saw him run a hand through his hair and adjust the bulge in his scrub pants. As if sensing she was looking at him, he turned around, giving her no time to suddenly duck further into the doorway. Doctor Tyler glared at her, but instead of his 'I'm in control' surgeon look, she could see the flush to his cheeks, and the slight flare of his nostrils, trying to still breathe in her arousal. Jade swallowed, then glanced down at the very evident swelling in the front of his scrubs. Doctor Tyler started walking towards her. Jade squealed, ducking further into the doorway and running into the surgical suite, stopping instantly when she saw the table and the doctors standing around it.

<u>PART 3</u>

Jade stared at the table, they left no pretence, the lights were already on and shining against the black padding. The glow was eerie yet exciting. Her instincts told her run, run far and run fast. But her body...her body craved their touch, their exams...no it craved his touch, his exam. A hand touched her lower back making her body jump, but she didn't take any steps towards the table. The hand moved slightly so the palm was against her hip, the fingers against her lower back.

"Hello Jade."

The voice was different than Doctor Tylers', yet was slightly familiar. However, her mind was still showing her the look on Doctors Tylers' face, as she peeked out from the doorway to look at him, making it impossible to place the voice now behind her. The fingers curled against her back and flattened out. Doctor Tyler walked around in front of her, blocking her view of the surgical table, but she still felt the hand. "I...I..."

"You what?" Doctor Kevin spoke lower, right behind her, he could feel the shivers down her spine. He had had her on the exam table once before, only once. She had been volunteered for the abdominal exam by her friend, in class. As his fingers had palpated the smooth skin of her abdomen, it had given him only a small glimpse, a small taste, of what Doctor Tyler had when she was on the surgical table naked before him.

"I...err...What are you going to do?" Jades heart beat hard, but she couldn't help crossing her legs, tensing her thighs as she did so they would brush against her already excited clit. she looked at Doctor Tyler, whose eyes moved down to her thighs. Surely he noticed what she was doing...oh how she wished it was his hand between her thighs. Doctor Tyler looked her in the eyes then brought the mask that was hanging around his neck up, so he could tie it onto his face. Jade felt the hand on the small of her back press a bit harder, encouraging her to step forward, but she stayed where she was. Her eyes on Doctor Tyler, as she waited for either him, or the voice behind her, to answer her question.

Doctor Kevin smiled and looked at Doctor Tyler who nodded back, the other doctors forming a horseshoe in front of her around him. "After medically examining every inch, and response, of your body, we will be teaching you a lesson; young lady."

Doctor Kevin looked over her shoulder, watching her breasts rise and fall with each breath she took, to no doubt try and calm her nerves. If only she wasn't wearing the hooded shirt, he bet her pink nipples would be hard and begging to be between the lips of her doctors...his lips as he suckled and flicked the tip of his tongue over the hardened nub. Watching her take a couple more breaths, he moved his hand lower on her back, his palm now bordering the top of her bare ass, his ring and pinky fingers teasing the area, reminding her that his hand could, at any moment, easily give her a swift spank to her bare bottom, or slip under the hooded shirt and pull it off her, leaving her completely naked. "Are you afraid?"

Jade bit her bottom lip, trying not to whimper. Looking at the masked faces looking back her, the stern look of Doctor Tylers eyes over his mask, and the glint of the surgical lights framing them from behind. It made her heart flutter and heat pool between her legs. Half of her wanted to jump up on the table, fill the need in her aching pussy and throbbing clit. The other half, was so intimidated by their power, their control, she either wanted to melt into a puddle for them or run like she never ran before. "No." The answer was weaker then she intended it to be.

Doctor Kevin brought his hand up her back and over her shoulder, wrapping it around her neck, pulling her body back into his. His other hand slid down her covered chest to her now presented pubic mound. Looking down her body he could see the subtle clenching of her thighs. he smiled behind his mask, he had no doubt that the moment his fingers moved between them, they would be covered in her silky wetness. "Spread your legs." He whispered the order in her ear. When she didn't move right away, doctor Kevin took a step back, bringing her body with him, making her chest arch back, her breasts poking up under the hoodie. The position pushing her hips forward, taking Jade a little off balance.

Jade leaned her shoulders back against the chest behind her. Taking a couple quick breaths, feeling his hand around her throat as she did. His grip wasn't tight enough to choke her, but was just enough to show her that she was his submissive, she was their patient...and it sent electric thrills to her clit. Jade swallowed against the palm. His simple step backward had forced her hips out towards the doctors all looking at her. His hand gripped tighter on her neck, warning her not to keep stalling. Glancing at Doctor Tyler she took a couple small steps, uncrossing and spreading her legs. Instantly the masked faces all looked down at her pussy. The shaved pink lips greeting them, no doubt glistening in the light spillage off the surgical lights. "Please!"

Doctor Kevin squeezed a bit harder as his other hand slid between her legs. His fingers found instant wetness. Hiding the moan behind his mask, he rubbed his fore and middle fingers against each other in the warm wetness, feeling the silky glide he had been so sure was going to be there. His cock hardened behind her, as Doctor Kevin knew he was directly responsible for some of this wetness on her labia. He shook his head, Jade was Doctor Tylers' patient, he had to remind himself of that. Although, that didn't mean he wouldn't get to make her moan and beg. Doctor Kevin gave her pussy a quick hard spank. SPANK. "You are already wet!" He kept his wrist against her pubic mound as he brought his hand up and down in another spank, this time curling his finger tips just inside of her slit. "Naughty girl!" He pulled back with his hand around her neck, pressing her against him more, showing her she had no means of escape, as he slowly rubbed his fingers in circles against her pussy. "Why are you so wet?" He felt the shivers move through her body as she was both embarrassed in front of the other doctors and turned on.

"I...I..." Jade glanced at Doctor Tyler but his eyes, along with every other doctor around him, were on her pussy and the doctors' hand that now touched it. His hand squeezed tighter making her swallow in reflex. "I can't tell you." The doctor behind her brought his hand out further and gave her three hard stinging spanks directly to her upper pussy and clit. SPANK. SPANK. SPANK. "Oooooow! Please!" The hand started rubbing slowly again, the sting tingling under the warm palm, and turning to heat in her clit causing her to want more.

"When I went to see her in her dorm, I caught her touching her clit, masturbating on her bed." Doctor Tyler looked at her squirming against Doctor Kevin's body. Her nipples were hidden behind her sweater, but he was sure they were budding. Her pussy was starting to turn a shade of red from Doctor Kevins' spankings. Doctor Tylers' cock was throbbing in his scrubs. Oh how he couldn't wait to hear her beg for him to let her cum. To hear her scream for him as he forced her to orgasm.

"Tell me now, young lady!" Doctor Kevin gave her pussy one more hard spank, SPANK. As her body jumped against him, he took a step back, forcing her body to arch more and present her now blushing pussy. Giving each thigh a spank to the inside forcing her to spread even more. SPANK. SPANK. She whimpered her hands coming up to his arm against her chest. "Hands down." He waited for her to slowly put her arms at her sides, her body having to rely on him for support. Using his forefinger and middle finger he spread her labia searching for her clit. As the little bud came into view he trapped it between his thumb and forefinger and pinched, not hard, but hard enough to make it swell with more excitement. "Tell me now!"

"She is getting wetter!" One of the doctors watching them pointed it out; Jade groaned.

Doctor Kevin pinched her clit harder making her jump, but the movement just caused him to keep squeezing. The pleasure turning into pain and pleasure mix. "Ooooohhh....."She bit her tongue to keep from saying anything. How could she tell them about the dream? "Please.....please I can't!"

Doctor Tyler walked up to her, sliding his hands up under her sweater, taking the material so it was high up, just under Doctor Kevins' hand at her throat, exposing her breasts. He was right, her pink nipples were erect and begging to be touched. Taking her nipples in his fingers he twisted slightly as he pinched them hard. "You can, and you will, Young lady!"

Pain shot straight down from her nipples to her clit which was already throbbing from being pinched. She could feel the wetness dripping down her leg, from the punishment and their dominance. She tried not looking at the surgeon but she couldn't help it. His eyes bore down into hers from his mask, forcing her to obey him, and adding to the juices flowing between her legs. "Ahhhhh..." She took a breath. Her body was overwhelmed with pleasure and pain at the same time, it didn't know what to register first. "I...I had a dream!" Jade hoped that would be enough, but they kept their hold on her most sensitive spots. She moaned, knowing full well, if she had been able, her hips would have bucked to try and brush her clit against the fingers that currently trapped and teased it.

"A dream about what?!" Doctor Tyler pinched her nipples a bit harder, just to watch her squirm and hear her moan. The sound full of submission and arousal he had no doubt every doctor in the room felt their cock twitch at hearing it.

Jade whimpered. "A dream about...." Jade swallowed, glancing at Doctor Tyler, then looking down towards the hand on her clit. "...about you...about your table...about the doctors here."

"It must have been very sexual." Doctor Kevin

said it, hoping it would add embarrassment calling her out on it in front of all the other doctors.

Jade still couldn't concentrate enough to place the voice of the doctor holding her. She couldn't believe she was telling them about her dream, but her nipples hurt, her clit was begging to be released and her slit was so wet, she had no choice but to submit and be their patient. "Yes doctor, it was."

"Did you have sex with Doctor Tyler in this dream?" The voice as low, so close to her ear she shivered at the aroused male tone.

Jade looked back up at Doctor Tyler, she was so embarrassed, she felt her face flush. "I...I...I wanted too."

"I doubt he would have turned you down, even in your dream." The voice almost laughed in her ear, then got very strict as Doctor Tyler glanced at the voice behind her. "What do you mean you wanted too?"

"I woke up before I could." Male laughter filled the room.

Doctor Tyler grinned behind his mask at the pout that was on Jades face. Releasing her nipples he stood back, taking a good look at her almost completely naked body. Oh he defiantly wouldn't have turned her down, in the waking, or the dream, world.

Doctor Kevin released her clit and gave her three hard spanks on it. SPANK. SPANK. SPANK. Her body shook against him, almost cuming from the pleasure and pain mix. "I think Doctor Tyler has been too lenient on you." Releasing her neck he used his body to push her up standing straight again. "We will change this together today." Placing his hands on her abdomen, he slid them up her body, feeling her nipples in the palm of his hands as he moved up. Reaching the sweater, that had slipped down just a bit she he had stood her up, he gripped the bottom and pulled up, causing her hands to come up and allowing him to slip the material from her body, leaving her completely exposed to everyone in the room. He watched as her hands twitched to cover up her breasts and pubic mound, but she put them back down at her sides. Although he would have loved to feel her ass cheek warm from the quick spank he would have given her, or hear the hitch in her breathing as he pinched her nipple for trying to hide it, he was impressed she was also cooperating. "Now, get your naughty ass on that surgical table! You are a disobedient patient, who needs to learn a good lesson from her doctors."

Jade looked at Doctor Tyler who had his arms crossed over his chest, he was more than ready to teach her a lesson. It made her heart flutter and heart pool between her legs. But she was so embarrassed he not only found her in her room, catching her day dreaming, but now he knew why. The doctors moved, forming a path towards the table.

Doctor Kevin put his hand on the nape of her

neck and whispered in her ear. "I told you once, you better cooperate or you'd find yourself on a different table." When she took a breath in, he knew she figured out who he was, but he was ok with that, it meant that whenever she was in his class her clit would always tingle, and her panties would always be wet. "Don't make me force you up onto it, you won't like the result."

Jade bit her bottom lip as she realised who had held her against his chest and exposed her pussy to the other doctors. She shouldn't be surprised but she was, and she thought about his hands as they moved across her abdomen in class, his finger tips dancing close to her pubic mound. His touch had lingered on her skin, not like Doctor Tyler's had, but it had still made her wet on the exam table. Doctor Kevin's voice made her shiver and she quickly moved towards the table, watching Doctor Tyler as she moved, wishing it had been his hand on her pussy. His fingers trapping her clit. His body she had been against.

<u>PART 4</u>

Jade stood next to the table, she could feel Doctor Kevin behind her, blocking her path from running. She put her hands against the black padding on the table then looked up at the bright lights, instantly squinting and looking away. Swallowing she looked across the table and saw Doctor Tyler standing across from her.

Doctor Tyler patted the table top. "You shouldn't keep your doctors waiting."

Jade licked her lips, her heart was beating so hard in her chest she was surprised she was able to even stand still. The wetness between her legs was growing just looking at him. His confidence and comfort, standing at the surgical table, adding to the control he held over her, making her stomach tighten and her clit tingle. But she couldn't let him remember that she had dreamed about him. That she had wanted him not only in her dreams, but that she was thinking about him while she touched herself, wishing it was his hand touching her and making her cum. Jade cleared her throat, leaning forward a bit against the table. "Why not? My doctors always keep me waiting." The doctors in the room all gasped and tisked her boldness, she knew she was in trouble.

"You let her speak to you this way Doctor Tyler?" Doctor Kevin took another step towards her, putting his one hand between her shoulder blades, forcing her down against the table a bit more and holding her in place, while his other hand came up and started spanking her bare ass. SPANK SPANK SPANK SPANK. The feel of her smooth bare skin against his palm felt good, and each spank added warmth to both her ass and his hand.

"No, each time she had shown attitude she has been punished." Doctor Tyler glared at her over his mask. Though he would love to be the one adding the sting to her bare butt cheeks, there was something about watching Doctor Kevin spank her. The way her body jumped as his hand connected with her ass, made her breasts jiggle, and nipples brush the surgical table as her body swayed with each spank. The soft whimpers as she bit her bottom lip, trying not to give in to the punishment and submit to their control. It all made his cock twitch in his scrub pants.

"Obviously she hasn't been punished or embarrassed enough!" SPANK SPANK SPANK. "Young lady! You never speak back to your doctors like that! I don't know how Doctor Tyler punished you in the past, but I will NOT let you get away with it, is that understood?!" Doctor Kevin lied, he had been in on her punishments, even took pleasure in embarrassing her in her classes. But he wasn't going to remind her of that. SPANK SPANK SPANK.

Jade whimpered, her ass starting to feel the sting of his spanks growing across both cheeks and even between her legs. She looked down at the table, trying not to give in. SPANK, "Ow!" She closed her eyes and wiggled her legs.

SPANK "Stand still!" Doctor Kevin watched as little dimples spread across her butt cheeks each time she clenched them hoping to somehow stop his palm from spanking her. SPANK

Jade couldn't help it, it was the only thing from keeping her from saying 'yes doctor.'

Doctor Tyler leaned across the table, placing his face against her cheek to whisper in her ear. "It would be far easier on you naughty girl, if you cooperated with your doctors."

Jade took a couple ragged breaths, she could feel his mask brushing against her cheek as his voice whispered in her ear. She leaned her head against him, "m...m...make...me." She felt the shiver run down her spine as he moaned low in her ear in response.

"As you wish." Doctor Tyler looked at Doctor Kevin. "Looks like she needs a bit more convincing." He leaned back so he could watch the reaction on her face.

Doctor Kevin forced a knee between Jade's legs and pushed them apart, tapping his knee against the inside of each of her knees, until she was spread wide enough that she had to lean against the surgical table for support. Keeping his one hand against her back, he brought the other slowly up the inside of her thigh.

Jade whimpered, taking a couple deep breaths, she could feel his hand sliding up against the sensitive area of her inner thighs. She knew he was going to touch her pussy, knew he was going to find her wet. But she also knew there was nothing she could do to stop him. She looked up at Doctor Tyler, instantly regretting it. Her knees going weak as she pictured his hand between her legs, teasing and threatening her.

Doctor Kevin stopped his hand at the crease of where her leg met her torso, the area already warm. "I have no doubt I am about to find her wet between her legs." The doctors moved around the table, each hoping to catch an early glimpse of her exposed pussy.

"Please...don't." Jade whimpered. She could feel her wetness trickling out of her, no doubt already onto the side of his glove.

Doctor Kevin leaned in close behind her. "Why not?"

Jade looked up at Doctor Tyler again and sighed. "I will get up on the table."

"Last thing you need right now young lady, is to get away with not listening to your doctors." Doctor Kevin brought his hand up against her pussy, giving her a quick SPANK, before he slid his fingers down and allowed two to slip inside of her.

Doctor Tyler watched as her jaw dropped at the surprise move, then her eyes close as she moaned the moment Doctor Kevin's fingers penetrated her. The look on her face made his cock jump. He wanted to make that look on her face as he thrust his cock deep and hard repeatedly into her. Claiming her orgasm as he forced her to cum.

"Just as I thought." Doctor Kevin wiggled his fingers within her, knowing that her soft moans were driving everyone in the room, including him and Doctor Tyler, up a wall. "A dirty naughty girl with a very wet pussy." He slid his fingers out a bit then moved them slowly back inside of her, making her moan low and moan the entire time it took for his fingers to go as deep as they possibly could. "Both that need a thorough examination and a lesson in obeying their doctor!" He quickly pulled his fingers from the heat of her vaginal canal and spanked her ass. SPANK. "Now! Get up on that table young lady."

Jade moaned in frustration. Frustration that she had to obey them. Frustration that it wasn't Doctor Tyler that had been inside of her. Frustration that Doctor Kevins fingers weren't still inside of her. Taking a breath she stood up and placed her hands flat against the table, the light from the surgical lights making them glow and reminding her that soon she would have nothing she could hide from them. She would be totally exposed to their control. Their touch. Their examinations. Their lessons.

<u>PART 5</u>

Jade took a breath then climbed up onto the surgical table. She couldn't believe she had given in and climbed up. Bringing her legs up so she was sitting, her feet against the table she looked around the room. The other doctors were now crowding closer to the table, no doubt taking up the best position possible to watch her body squirm under their control. Doctor Tyler stood to her right and she was trying her best not to look at him, other than in her peripheral vision. If she did look at him, she knew the wetness between her legs would grow and something told her if either him or Doctor Kevin found out, she would be punished.

Doctor Kevin moved towards the end of the table, looking at her. "Lie down young lady."

Jade chewed on her bottom lip. If she laid back she would be submitting to them, she would be opening up her body to whatever Doctor Tyler and Doctor Kevin could think of. She looked around again, turning her head over her shoulder her gaze instantly stopped on the anesthesia machine behind her. She closed her eyes. Whether or not she laid back against the surgical table, they could definitely make her do it. She was tempted to tell them, to dare them, to make them force her against the table. She could feel the words on the tip of her tongue as she looked back at Doctor Kevin. But the glare he was giving her over his mask made a shiver run down her spine. Slowly she moved back onto her elbows then to her back. Doctor Kevin wrapped his hands around her ankles and pulled her feet out towards him making her squeal in surprise.

"Next time when I give you an order to do something, do it faster." Doctor Kevin let her ankles go.

Jade closed her eyes as the bright lights shone down towards her. In the back of her mind she had her suspicions they were a distraction. A hand touched her abdomen making her sigh as the warmth and slight pressure felt good. Prying one eye open to find out who it was she saw Doctor Tyler standing right next to her, his bare palm against her stomach. Her heart started beating harder and she hoped he couldn't feel it against his palm. Although, if it made him forget about her telling him she had dreamt about him touching her, examining her, filling her with his cock, she might be ok with her body giving away her current excitement.

Doctor Tyler moved his hand from her body taking her right arm and placing it against the arm board, restraining it to the table. He looked down at her as Doctor Kevin moved up to her left side, taking her arm and restraining it. She was staring at him, her breathing getting faster. He couldn't help the way his eyes moved down the line of her neck, watching as her breasts moved with each breath she was trying to hide. Her nipples already budding. The soft curve of her rib cage moving down to her stomach, her belly button twisting a bit as she bent one leg and moved her hips side to side. She was definitely aroused, the movement of her hips and thighs likely brushing her clit. Oh how he wanted to slide his hand between her thighs, feel how hot she was. Let his fingertips touch her silky wetness.

Jade looked at each arm, testing the restraints but they had tied them tight. She looked back up at Doctor Tyler, her body felt hot and she could feel her excitement seep out and possibly onto the table. Oh how she hoped he wouldn't notice. But as she looked at him in his scrubs and mask her vaginal core felt empty. She wanted him to fill her, needed him to fill her. She did her best to hide a moan as she moved her legs. With any luck she could wipe away at least some of her wetness, and hopefully ease the tingling in her clit.

Doctor Kevin grinned behind his mask, he could see Doctor Tyler's eyes scanning her body, not that he blamed him. They were both wishing their hands, and possibly other body parts, could follow the path of his eyes. Her body enticing, begging to be examined, explored, and controlled. Oh he was looking forward to making her scream with pleasure. Though he wasn't sure how long Doctor Tyler would let him discipline her body before he took over to dominate her. "You are squirming a lot young lady."

Jade swallowed, stopping her hips moving for a moment, until she felt a trickle of wetness flow out of her. She twisted her hips to brush her clit and hopefully stop some of her excitement. "I...I can't help it."

Doctor Kevin nodded. "Sounds like you have a lot of trouble controlling these urges of yours, naughty girl. First your dream about Doctor Tyler here, and you touching yourself as you fantasize being on his table in front of all these doctors. And now that you are on our surgical table...." He glared at her, quickly learning that the simple look caused her cheeks to blush a soft pink, her nipples to bud and with the way her hips were now moving, and he guessed her clit to tingle. "Think we will have to restrain you a bit further." He moved down towards her hip, putting a hand on her left hip and patting it as she kept squirming.

Jade moaned. She knew if he restrained her legs he wouldn't do it with them closed. Which meant he would be able to see her wetness. "No!...please!" She looked down at him then up at Doctor Tyler, feeling her stomach quiver as she did.

Doctor Kevin let his hand slide from her hip, down her leg, slowly, seductively. Even as she moved he followed the soft lines of her thigh down to her calf. When he reached her ankle he grabbed it and pulled it up towards the leg restraints.

Jade had felt his hand moving down her body, doing her best not to moan. His palm had been soft against her, yet firm with the confidence of likely hundreds of previous exams. Although she was pretty sure they didn't teach that kind of touch or exam in medical school, at least she hadn't seen anyone teach it yet. But the moment he took her ankle panic set in. Jade pulled back against his hold.

"Don't fight me naughty girl, you won't like the punishment from doing so!" Doctor Kevin looked at her, gripping her ankle a bit tighter. Jade pulled back against his force, causing him to suddenly lose his grip. The lack of resistance caused her to kick forward hitting Doctor Kevin square in the chest. Doctor Kevin gasped and fell back onto the stool coughing as the wind was knocked out of him. The doctors in the room came closer, a couple moving up to him.

Jade started moving again, twisting her hips and legs together. Doctor Tyler put his hand on her chest, between her breasts, sliding it up to her neck, forcing her chin up. His eyes stared into hers. He didn't grip hard enough to choke her but it was close. "That, was a mistake young lady!"

Jade looked at him, though she was afraid of the power he was currently showing her, it was also turning her on. She could feel her pussy was so wet there had to be a spot on the surgical table. Thankfully, her legs would block the surgical lights from shinning on it and really letting the doctors, especially Doctor Tyler, know how excited she was. His hand gripped tighter around her neck, and part of her couldn't help but wonder if he was getting turned on by holding her down.

"Knock her out." Doctor Kevin gasped. "I'll punish her once I get her fully restrained."

Jades eyes went wide as she looked at Doctor Tyler, but he just tilted his wrist upwards, forcing her chin to move up and into the perfect position for the black mask heading for her face. She tried moving her head, but it just caused him to grip tighter. "Bad girl." Doctor Tyler almost growled it. Jade felt the soft rubber cover her face, and could hear the hiss of the gas as it flowed high to take her out. She hated to feel whatever Doctor Kevin was going to have in store for her when she came too, but Doctor Tylers' hand and the look in his eyes as he glared at her over his mask made her...made her feel...Jade tried to keep her legs tightly pressed together but with each breath she felt her body relaxing. She blinked up at Doctor Tyler, but he never took his eyes off of her. She felt her legs relax against the table parting slightly as they did. Blinking again, she took another breath, trying to keep Doctor Tyler in focus, but she couldn't. As her eyes closed she heard Doctor Tyler scold her once more. "Bad girl."

<u>PART 6</u>

Doctor Tyler watched as she struggled to keep her eyes open. No matter how much she would try to fight it, the anesthetic would win. He had seen it before. More so in men really, trying to beat the system, show how tough they are. If they could have seen past his mask they would have seen the small smirk on his face as the anesthesiologist either turned up the gas or took out another syringe. Their faces would relax and then their bodies relax, doctors 1, patient 0. But there was something different about this time. He could feel the way the muscles in her neck tried to fight against his hold, could feel the nipple of her right breast brush against his forearm with each breath she at first took in fear, then tried to hold. The hiss of the machine adding to the scolding the other doctors were whispering around the table. Her eyes, hmm yes it was her eyes. They were big, wide eyed as though sacred were also excited. The hazel irises seductive and they never left his. Even as she blinked, when they opened, they stared right back at his. As the gas took over they clouded a bit but he could always see her desire for him. His cock swelling as she wanted him even in her drugged mind. Doctor Tyler felt her neck relax against his palm, her chin now resting against his hand he slowly released his grip, letting it rest just below her collar bone. "Bad girl." She was out, but he had no doubt she still heard him. He watched her breasts rise and fall, her nipples slowly relaxing, they wouldn't stay that way for long though, not once she was awake. He grinned. His eyes moved down to her pelvic region, her thighs slightly parted now that her body was relaxed. His cock twitched as she made a soft moan, the rubber mask muffling it, but he still heard it. Holding her down, forcing her head up for the mask, the power he had, the control he had over her, and the submission in her eyes, the excitement and fear from his control. It all made his cock pulse for more. He had to know. He had to know if the submission and excitement had gone between her legs. He had to know if the muffled moan in the mask was residual need. Taking a breath he slid his hand between her thighs, parting them a bit further. His own eyes closed for a moment as her silky wetness coated his fingers. He felt pre cum leak out of the tip of his cock.

"Get the leg restraints ready and put her in them."

Doctor Kevin's order to the doctors made Doctor Tyler groan in frustration. He had been in inside of her before as they took her out before releasing her from his table. But now he wanted to know what it would feel like to be inside of her as she woke up. Hmm what would it have felt like to be inside of her when she had the dream about him? Would her body wrap around his shaft? Would it still milk him for everything he had? His hand moved as her legs were pulled apart and forced into to the restraints, opening her hips wide as they were strapped down. She moaned in the mask again, her sedation slightly lighter than he expected. But was she dreaming of him again? What would it be like if he let the tip of his cock tease her entrance? Would she get wetter? Would she moan again? How relaxed would her body be? Would it stay relaxed? What if he let his cock slowly slide inside of her. Would her muscles grip him tighter? Feeling him penetrate her even in sleep and draw him deeper? What would the look on her face be when the mask was removed? Hmmmm he could picture her biting her lower lip, her head moving side to side as she dreamt about him. As she felt him. Doctor Kevin sat on the stool, he could easily walk up to him and push him away from the surgical table, take his cock out of his scrubs and thrust deep inside of her. It was so tempting...his thumb rubbed the fingers of his hand, her wetness still covering them. He wanted to feel the wetness over his cock, feel it covering his shaft, allowing him to slide in and out of her deeper and deeper until her body shook and gripped him tight as she came for him. Came because of him.

Doctor Tyler cleared his throat and looked back at Jade as the anesthesiologist removed the mask, allowing her to start to wake up. He looked at Doctor Kevin. "I know you will punish her, but remember doctor, she is mine." It was taking all of his strength not to push Doctor Kevin out of the way and take her right there on the table.

Doctor Kevin nodded. He knew that all too well, had seen her squirm under the surgeons control and beg for release many times before. Even seen him punish her for disobeying him. But right now it was his turn to teach her a lesson. To remind her who was in control of her body. And who it was she needed to submit too.

<u>PART 7</u>

Doctor Kevin looked at Doctor Tyler then around to the other doctors watching. "You know, she puts on a brave face, let's see what happens when she wakes up and no one is here."

Doctor Tyler looked at her body, her breasts slowly rising, her nipples relaxing after no touch to her body. "Interesting idea of punishment, and you said I was going easy on her."

Doctor Kevin grinned behind his mask. "Oh my plans for her are far from over. I just realized I need to play with her mind, let her know that she has absolutely no control." He glanced up at Doctor Tyler as he moved away from the table. "Something you have been giving too much to her."

Doctor Tyler glared at Doctor Kevin. He may have allowed her to touch herself while he watched after she dreamt of him, but it was his control and power that she had been dreaming of in the first place. Doctor Kevin was walking on a thin line.

Doctor Kevin ushered the other doctors behind the table out of her sight and placed a finger over his mask, making sure no one made a sound.

****

Jade moaned, her mind still feeling a hand sliding down her thigh. She could feel her clit tingling, oh how she wanted to touch it, to think of

Doctor Tyler...but last time she did he had been watching her, and then he....wait a second. Her eyes shot open and she saw the surgical light. Jade took a breath and looked between her legs, expecting to see either Doctor Kevin or Doctor Tyler...but no one was there.

Blinking she looked back up at the light and closed her eyes, she had to be dreaming? She twisted her hands in the restraints, but they were solid. She looked back up at the light then turned her head side to side, looking for someone, anyone...but there was no one. No green or blue scrubs, no eyes looking down at her from their masks. Her heart raced. Surely they wouldn't leave her alone in the surgical suite would they? In the hidden areas of the school. She took another breath, maybe the anesthesiologist was still there. She tilted her head as far back as the restraints would allow her body to move, but she only saw the equipment.

She relaxed her body back against the table and looked down. Her legs were still spread wide, exposed to anyone who might walk into the room. She bit her bottom lip, her heart starting to pound in her chest. "Hello?!" She tried closing her legs, but the stirrups wouldn't let her move. She felt wetness trickle down her labia. She could still picture Doctor Kevin's glare between them, after she kicked him. She let out another breath, trying to calm herself down. Maybe they did leave her there as punishment. Swallowing she looked around the room again, her hands continuing to twist in the restraints as the cold operating room air brushed over her naked body.

Looking down she saw her belly button bounce slightly as her heart raced. She wasn't sure if she was more scared that the doctors had left, or disappointed. Her clit wanted Doctor Tyler to touch it, examine it, make it swell and cum. And when she could see him, even if it was just him next to the table, or when he placed his hand on her body to examine her or warn her to behave, it made her stomach flutter and her juices flow knowing he could at any time force her to orgasm. She swallowed again, "hello?! Anyone there?" Her voice echoed in the operating room.

Jade started to panic. Her arms and wrists pulling at the restraints as her head moved side to side looking for someone, anyone. "Let me go!!" Her eyes glanced between her legs. At this point she would even be relieved to see Doctor Kevin between her knees, even knowing he would punish her. "Please!" Her chest started rising and falling faster as the panic made her breathe faster, her breasts bouncing as she did. Jade pulled at the restraints again and started to scream. "Let me g...." A hand covered her mouth, instantly gagging her.

Doctor Kevin pressed his hand firmly over her mouth. He could feel her breath against his fingers as she looked up, trying to see him. "Bad girl." He whispered it into her ear. Standing up he looked down at her, his hand still covering her mouth. Jade felt goosebumps shiver along her spine as he stared down from his mask. "Just like this morning, when you thought you were alone and Doctor Tyler found you touching yourself, masturbating, thinking of him, you were not alone. Something you need to remember from now on young lady." He loosened his grip on her face, and nodded to one of the doctors who came up to her side.

Jade glanced over at him and saw the needle in his hand. She screamed against Doctor Kevins hand, but the doctor had no mercy. She felt the doctor press on her skin, looking for the right vein, the cold wet alcohol swab, then watched as the tip of the needle pressed into her skin, breaking the barrier and sliding deeper. She looked back at Doctor Kevin.

"Relax, it's just an IV, gives me more control." He glanced at the doctor who secured the IV in place then back at Jade, letting his hand move from her mouth.

"Let me go!"

Doctor Kevin raised his eye brows. "Really, even after you thought you were alone, strapped to a surgical table, you are going to fight me?"

Jade took a couple breaths then nodded. "Yes." Her fight or flight would have her fight, even if her clit wanted her to beg to have the surgeon, beg to even have Doctor Kevin, between her legs.

"Yes what?!"

Jade swallowed, looking at him, she could hear the other doctors moving around the table.

"Sounds like a certain bad girl still needs to learn a lesson." He reached down and took her right nipple between his thumb and forefinger, pinching and pulling up as he talked. "Yes what, young lady?!"

Jade bit her lip trying not to give in, but he kept pinching harder and harder. "Ahhh...yes doctor!"

Doctor Kevin released her nipple, his hand moving down between her legs, as he moved down the table. "I'm willing to bet that even now, you are a naughty girl and if let my fingers slip between your legs I will find you wet." He grinned behind his mask. "But then again, maybe I should have Doctor Tyler take a look."

Jade gasped and watched as Doctor Tyler walked beside the table and moved between her legs. She wanted to look away, but she couldn't. She wanted him to touch her so much, she needed to watch him do it just to make sure that it was actually him.

Doctor Tyler snapped on a glove, his eyes staring back at hers. He could already see her pink labia were glistening, but he wanted to watch her squirm in embarrassment as he exposed her to the other doctors. Sitting down on the stool a couple of the doctors moved in to look over his shoulder. Jade groaned, but she couldn't look away. Doctor Tyler looked down at her pussy, her puffy lips, and clit poking out from under its hood told him she wanted him to touch her. The small trickle of wetness from her slit, onto the surgical table, made his cock swell and twitch, knowing that she too wanted him to burry himself deep inside of her. His fingers pulled apart her labia, his thumbs slid down to her slit and put pressure, watching as her muscles contracted, wanting him to push inside of her, begging him to fill her. He looked up at Doctor Kevin. "Oh yes, she is very wet."

Jade followed his gaze to Doctor Kevin, her eyes going wide as she saw the syringe in his hand. "No! Hey, wait!" She tried moving her body away from Doctor Kevin but the restraints kept her in position. She started pulling on them. "Don't!....let me go?!"

Doctor Kevin grinned behind his mask. "Young lady, you are going to learn not to fight your doctor one way or the other. And judging by the kick you gave me, you need to learn it the hard way." He looked at her then to the syringe as he depressed the plunger, allowing the clear liquid to flow into her veins. "Don't worry, it is just a little versed. Think of it as a little pre insurance to help you relax and make sure you don't fight what I have planned for you."

Jade felt her heart pound as Doctor Kevin took the syringe and placed it on the counter behind him. She had no idea what he had planned but she was...she was...she blinked, taking a breath she felt her body relax against the table. "Won't...work."

Doctor Kevin laughed, placing his hand against

her abdomen, feeling her body relax under his palm. "Young lady, it already is."

Jade could hear the chuckles from the other doctors around the table. "Wh...wh...what are you planning on doing?" She took a deeper breath, feeling the warmth of his palm against her skin, as her stomach rose and fell under it. She wasn't tired enough to sleep but she felt very relaxed.

Doctor Tyler placed his thumb on her clit and started to rub it slowly, while Doctor Kevin slid his hand further up her chest, so it rested between her breasts. "I'm going to take you to a place where you can't fight back, but you can feel everything that is happening to you."

Jade looked back at Doctor Tyler. Every small circle on her clit made it tingle and heat grow between her legs. She moaned softly then looked back at Doctor Kevin. "H...how?"

Doctor Kevin smiled and took a syringe out of the top pocket of his scrubs. He watched her eyes go wide as he uncapped the needle and showed her the white drug inside. "With this." Jade started breathing a little faster. " I can tell by the look on your face you remember this from your classes as propofol." He took the IV line in his hand and held it so the syringe was inserted but he hadn't delivered the drug yet. "And I can tell by the look in your eyes you would have tried to fight the drug too. That is why you got a small dose of the versed a head of time, young lady. You will learn to obey your doctor. To not fight the control he has over your body and its responses."

Jade whimpered as she watched him press the plunger and the milky white fluid fill the IV tubing. Her eyes following it as it moved down closer and closer to her arm. She wanted to even just pull on the restraints but her body was relaxed and wouldn't listen to her brain to struggle. She glanced up at Doctor Kevin then back at her arm as the white propofol reached her arm and moved into her body. Jade bit her tongue, trying to fight it, looking down at Doctor Tyler. His finger felt so good against her clit. She could feel her hips starting to move. Her eyes closed as a sudden wave of tiredness washed over her body. She felt heavy, like she couldn't move it without a bunch of effort, but the feeling of Doctor Tylers touch made her whole body tingle, not just her clit.

Doctor Kevin slid his hand down to her abdomen, sliding his palm back and forth over her stomach, feeling her body give in to the drug, and listening to the soft moans his touch caused her to do as she fell deeper into the drugs spell.

<u>PART 8</u>

Doctor Kevin watched as Jades' head moved to the side slightly, her neck relaxing as her stomach did beneath his hand. It was going to make his plans much easier but he wasn't going to let her slip completely under the spell of the sedatives. Oh no, far from it. He planned on making sure she still felt what he was doing, she just wouldn't be able to fight it, fight him. Doctor Kevin looked up at the anesthesiologist, "don't let her sleep, keep her consciously sedated." The doctor nodded.

Jade felt something sticky on her shoulders and then around her breasts. Her chest rising and falling slowly. She could feel the surgical table beneath her, her body seemed to melt into it. Her brain told her that she should still fight, that Doctor Kevin still had yet to punish her. But her body felt so relaxed, it was no longer hers to control. It was strictly Doctor Kevins' and Doctor Tylers' to own. To deliver mercy, pleasure, or punishment. She moaned then heard a soft beep in the back ground. Her eyebrows furrowed and she licked her lips, focusing on the beep. What was it? Why hadn't she heard it before?

Doctor Kevin looked at Doctor Tyler who reluctantly stood up off the stool between her legs, allowing Doctor Kevin to sit back down. Doctor Kevin slid his hand down to the top of her pubic mound then patted it gently. Taking a pair of gloves off the nearby stand he snapped on one then the other, lacing his fingers to make sure the latex fit him perfectly. He didn't want his gloves to be so loose he would feel the material ridge and rub against his hand. No. He wanted to be able to just feel her. Her heat, her softness, her muscles. Sitting down between her legs he looked at the other doctors. "Now gentlemen. Though we know Doctor Tyler has been inside of her, filling her vaginal canal, we don't know if she has had intercourse with anyone else. Therefore, we don't know how tight she really is." Doctor Tyler cleared his throat. "Well, Doctor Tyler has some idea." The doctors chuckled. "And I owe this young lady some punishment." He put his hand on her pussy, covering it. His finger tips pressing against her clit. "Jade...Jade can you hear me?"

The beeping got faster as a jolt of pleasure shot from between her legs. She moaned, feeling something pressing against her clit. Taking another breath she heard the beeps more clearly...

"Jade...Jade!" He gave her pussy a firm spank. SPANK. Her body jumped, and he watched as a trickle of wetness dripped onto the surgical table. He smiled, the more her body got excited, the easier this was going to be. "Answer me naughty girl!"

Her mind was still a little foggy, and she tried pulling her wrists against the restraints but her body didn't move. Doctor Kevins' voice shot through the haze and she felt the sting of his spanking awaken her clit even more. "Hmmmm, yes doctor."

"Good." Taking two fingers he pressed against her slit, rubbing them to coat them in her wetness. "What are you feeling young lady?" Though he didn't want her fully awake, he also wanted to make sure she didn't pass out on him, and making her talk helped him judge the fine line.

"Hmmm... tired." Jade heard chuckles from around her.

"I can imagine. Tell me, if you feel this...?" Doctor Kevin took his two fingers, pressed the tips against her vaginal entrance then thrust them forward quickly.

Jade gasped, her body moving with the thrust. She had felt his fingers pressing, forcing their way slowly into her, but the quick motion of them sliding deep inside of her took her brain a second to register. "Yes..."

Doctor Kevin rotated his wrist, letting his fingers slide in a circle around her core. She felt warm, his fingers slippery even inside of her, and he couldn't help but wonder how it was going to feel when his entire fist was inside of her. "Yes what?"

Jade groaned, "yes doctor."

"Good girl." Doctor Kevin slid his fingers out to the second knuckle then slowly pushed them back in. He had found out from his first thrust, that if he went fast, she wouldn't feel it right away, and he needed to punish her for kicking him. And if he were to be honest, he wanted to see her struggle. Watch her breasts jiggle, her labia get pink and puffy, and catch the scent of her excited womanhood, something he knew everyone else in the room was waiting for. Taking his fingers out he kept his hand horizontal, opposite the normal stretch of a speculum, and pressed in with three fingers, forcing her body to open up a bit more.

Jade moaned. She could feel her slit stretch, and couldn't believe how wet she was getting from it. From feeling his fingers fill her. "Hmmmmm Doctor...."

Doctor Kevin grinned behind his mask. She would get some pleasure in the long run, but this was meant as a punishment. She was going to learn that she was his patient, that she was their patient. And that her pleasure was theirs to give. If she disobeyed or fought them, that she would be punished. "Now, I'm going to ask Doctor Tyler to help me. Up to you if you want to put on some gloves." Doctor Tylers cock was throbbing in his scrubs, wanting to be where Doctor Kevins fingers currently were. "Now gentlemen, the reason I sedated her was to help relax her body and muscles. Though she is quite wet, having her relaxed will help me slide my entire fist into her, but allow her to still feel everything. You might want to move in closer to watch as her body is forced to open up for me." Doctor Kevin glanced up at Jade as she looked down her body at him. "Doctor Tyler, to help keep her well lubricated, I'm going to get you to expose and play with her clit. Not enough to let her cum, least right away, this is a punishment for a naughty girl after all." He smiled when Jade moaned at his scolding.

Doctor Tyler opted not to put on gloves, he wanted to feel her body. Feel the smooth skin of her labia as his thumb and middle finger spread them apart, allowing his forefinger to find her clit. A couple of the doctors took a breath as her clit swelled under Doctor Tyler's touch. He used his thumb to pull back the rest of her clit hood and fully expose her clit. Her body jumped as he stroked it then lightly squeezed it. Doctor Kevin's fingers were instantly covered in wetness, the latex shining in the surgical light. Doctor Tyler groaned. His cock was hard, his scrubs barely able to hold his own excitement.

Doctor Kevin smiled. Taking four fingers at her entrance he pushed inwards, her body tensed a bit but the sedation kept her muscles from holding him back.

Jade groaned, her pussy stretching. It hurt but also felt good. The combination causing her to get so wet she could feel coolness between her legs.

"Now young lady." Doctor Kevin twisted his fingers around, trying to prepare her body for the invasion of his fist, watching as Doctor Tyler's fingers stroked and trapped her clit. Each stroke caused her muscles to move as though to draw his fingers deeper inside of her. "You will learn never to fight your doctor, especially kicking him! That was very bad!!"

The doctors around her spread legs all murmured their agreement. It made her feel embarrassed which was an interesting mix with the sedatives and the pleasure pain between her legs. The beeping was getting faster, as Doctor Tyler's fingers sent pleasure shooting throughout her body and her heart racing.

"And bad girls need to be punished." Doctor Kevin slid his thumb in towards his palm and pushed his fingers against her slit, going slow, making sure she felt the pressure building against her body.

Jade moaned, her hips bucking just a bit as she felt her body start to stretch, she thought it would stop, but it only increased. Her vaginal core forced to open wider with each little push. She stared panting, pain starting to wake her from the sedation. Doctor Tyler's fingers pinched her clit causing her hips to buck and her muscles to grip onto Doctor Kevin's fingers pulling him deeper.

Doctor Kevin took advantage of the moment, pushing his hand deeper. The doctors around him were breathing hard, almost matching his patient as she started to scream a little with the stretching. Her pussy so wet the table and drape under her were soaking, her arousal filling the room. His hand was half way in. "Still have more to go naughty girl. You will take my entire fist inside of you." Doctor Kevin could feel a wet spot in his own scrubs. Her body felt so warm, he couldn't wait to feel it around his entire hand. "Your body is mine. It is Doctor Tylers'. It is ours to pleasure and to punish." He started pushing his hand in deeper again.

Jade screamed, her body moving a bit more on the table, the sedation nearly worn off. She could feel his fingers sliding deeper, spreading out, forcing her body to open wider. It hurt, it seemed to even sting a little, as it stretched, but it felt so good. Her clit tingled and throbbed with every touch. Her body wrapped around Doctor Kevin's hand. She stared panting. "Ahhhhh, hmmmmm...ooooh please, please."

"No. Whatever it is, no. You were very uncooperative and a dirty naughty girl. You need to get taught a lesson." Doctor Kevin kept sliding his hand slowly inside of her, forcing her to feel everything. Her wetness was now dripping down his glove and onto his forearm. All the doctors eyes were glued to her slit, watching as Doctor Kevin's hand spread and filled her.

Jade groaned, and let out a gasp as she felt his hand suddenly slip inside of her. Her muscles wrapped around his wrist.

Doctor Kevin curled his fingers inside of her to make a true fist. "Hmmm good girl." Keeping his fist inside of her he gently pumped his arm in and out a bit, making sure she felt him filling her inside. Looking up at her, he pulled his wrist back, keeping a tight fist, so that just the edge of his fist was at her entrance, teasing that it would come out. He smiled behind his mask as he slowly pushed it forward. "And now young lady. With everyone watching, and my fist inside of you, you will cum."

Jade moaned. "Noooo, please!! I can't!"

Doctor Kevin nodded to one of the doctors who reluctantly took his eyes of the glistening wet pussy. "You have no choice but to relax now and let it happen."

Jade turned her head and watched as the doctor depressed the syringe into her IV, the white creamy drug moving down the tube into her arm. She panted, "no...please....I...I..." the fast beeps started to calm down a bit. Jade took a breath, her body relaxing around Doctor Kevin's fist. She could still feel him, feel him twist his wrist, or wiggle his fingers inside of her. She just couldn't hold back any pleasure it was also giving her.

Doctor Tyler rubbed and twirled her clit, his tongue wanting to be the one on her body, to taste the sweet juices flowing from her pussy. His cock was rock hard, and each moan she did, each low seductive submissive moan, caused more pre cum to leak out from the head.

Doctor Kevin started pumping his fist in and out a bit, feeling her body grip his wrist with each small slide. The movements, even if they were small, were heard throughout the room. Her excitement covering everything, making a wet sucking noise, begging for more. "Get ready young lady. Your body will orgasm. You will learn that your doctor has complete control over your body, not you." He thrust his hand deep inside of her, pulling back just enough that when he rotated his wrist, he let two fingers in his fist curl out and stroke her G spot. Her body jumped as did her heart rate. The monitor beeping rapidly, catching his attention for just a moment before the muscles around his wrist contracted and brought his gaze back to her pussy, penetrated by his hand. Doctor Tyler moaned along with her as he pinched her clit and rubbed it in a circle at the same time. "Cum right now young lady."

Jade panted, moaning. She wanted to fight it, but the drug kept her in submission, and her body was so turned on. She could hear how wet she was, could even feel it as it trickled out of her and onto the surgeon. The pressure on her clit sent waves of pleasure and combining it with her G spot.... Jades hips bucked, her body tensed and she screamed as she came hard, squirting all over Doctor Kevins' scrubs as she did.

Doctor Kevin kept pumping his fist as she came, the other doctors moving away to relieve some tension in their scrubs.

Doctor Tyler looked at Doctor Kevin. He was unsure of what to say. Part of him wanted to high five the other surgeon for teaching her a lesson in a creative way, while another part wanted to punch his lights out for making his patient cum so hard she squirted.

Jade panted, feeling Doctor Kevin's fist as he slowly pulled it out. Her slit completely soaked. Her muscles helping to push him out a little bit. But as his fist pulled back it stretched her open again. She moaned, the sedation helping to keep her calm, but she could feel every part of his hand slide out of her. As the widest part of his fist finally slipped out, the rest followed quickly.

Doctor Tyler watched as her pussy continued to contract its muscles, both relieved the invader was gone and disappointed. Oh how he needed to be inside of her. To make her feel him as he came deep inside of her.....

<u>PART 9</u>

Jade moaned low. She could feel the wetness between her legs, the little trickle that still flowed every time her vaginal muscles contracted. Her body felt tired, relaxed, her slit was sore but was still craving more. Taking a breath she forced herself to open her eyes and look up. Her fingers flexed in the restraints. She refused to give in to the tiredness. She refused to give in to Doctor Kevin....and she refused to give in to her surgeon, Doctor Tyler. Her stomach was sore from tensing and cuming so hard, from feeling her entrance stretch and take Doctor Kevin's entire fist. Yet her vaginal core still waved for more. Still craved to feel Doctor Tyler's cock deep inside of her, the thought only adding to the wetness between her legs. Jade did her best to focus on the soreness of her muscles, it was the only way to keep her from begging the doctors to have mercy on her. Beg them to give her pleasure.

Doctor Kevin snapped off his gloves and looked up at Jade from between her legs. "Have you learned a lesson young lady?"

Jade licked her lips. Her mind a mix of needing Doctor Tyler to fill her, to change the feeling of Doctor Kevin's fist inside of her to his cock. To feel her body wrap around him. Feel him pulse and throb as he came inside of her...but she also didn't want to give in to Doctor Kevin. "Yes..."

"What is that?" Doctor Kevin stood up and

walked to her hip standing across from Doctor Tyler.

Jade took a breath, looking up at him, doing her best to look straight into his eyes staring down at her from his surgical mask. "That your fist actually fits inside of me." The corners of her lips turned up into a semi smile as the other doctors burst out laughing, not expecting her to be defiant.

Doctor Tyler was glad he had a mask on as it hid his own grin. Doctor Kevin had accused him of being too soft on Jade. It was good to see her still take on an attitude even after he punished her. Plus, truth be told, he took pleasure in Doctor Kevin's embarrassment simply because Doctor Kevin had made his patient cum and cum hard. That was his job. He was the one to make her beg, pant and scream, not Doctor Kevin.

Doctor Kevin shook his head. "You're asking for it young lady." Doctor Kevin wrapped his hand around the surgical light handle, pulling it down and angling it towards her. The monitor beeped loudly as the simple motion that he had done countless times in surgery caused her heart to race in fear. Oh yes, she may act tough, but in the end, she was strapped to the surgical table. She was his and Doctor Tyler's patient. Looking down at her he took a pair of gloves off the nearby table and put them on, lacing his fingers together to fit the latex gloves more tightly to his hands. "Hmmmmm." She stared back him, her bottom lip lightly quivering. Doctor Kevin turned towards the table and picked up a scalpel then turned back to her, holding it up so the metal shined in the surgical light, looking at the scalpel, giving her time to focus on it. Doctor Kevin then looked back down at her. "Perhaps you would like to play real a game of operation?"

Jade did her best to keep her heart from leaping out of her chest the moment she saw the scalpel in his hand, but as he looked down at her she felt it pound. Heard the monitor giving away her fear as it beeped in time to her thumping heart. Her eyes were glued to his hand and the knife. He moved towards her body, his hand getting slowly closer and closer. Jade bit her tongue, she refused to give in...she....she....oh gawd, he wouldn't really touch her body with it would he?....she watched his fingers move against the handle, the small movement purely muscle memory from surgeries before...Jade panicked. "No! Please...I.....I..."

Doctor Kevin stopped, the blade hovering just over her stomach. "No?"

Jade groaned. "No doctor, I...I...I...am sorry." She licked her lips again.

Doctor Kevin looked up at Doctor Tyler. "She can learn." He never would have actually cut her, but there was more to dominance and submission than purely restraints and touching. No, there was defiantly a strong mental aspect, and as a dominant, as a doctor, you weren't truly in control, until you had your patient fully focused on you and your control.

Doctor Tyler nodded. His cock was rock hard in his scrubs. Her scent filled the operating room. Her nipples still budding and erect from coming so hard, her skin still blushing pink from her recent orgasm. He could just imagine the feeling if her naked chest against his. Could almost feel the beat of her racing heart against him as his hips thrust into her. Feel the warmth of her breath against his neck as he laid on top of her, his fingers laced in hers as he pinned her arms above her head. Good gawd, the next time he found her masturbating in her dorm room he was going to rip off his clothes and claim her. Force her hands above her head, push her knees further open, and slide the head of his cock to her entrance. And just as she started to protest, he would wrap his lips around hers and thrust deep and hard inside of her, stealing her screams of pleasure as he kissed her and filled her vaginal core.

Doctor Kevin waved a hand in front of Doctor Tyler's face. "Doctor?..." When the surgeon looked up at him Doctor Kevin smirked. "What do you think, doctor?"

Doctor Tyler glanced at the monitors and then Jades naked body. "I think you've worn her out doctor." Doctor Tyler, nor his throbbing cock, were impressed. "I believe she needs time to recuperate." Jades soft sigh told him he was right but only added to the throbbing in his scrubs. Oh he might release her from his table, but it was simply to relieve Doctor Kevin from examining his patient. Doctor Tyler wasn't really about to let his cock go without feeling her hot core wrap right around it, milking it for everything. Oh no...that would never happen. Doctor Tyler looked up at the anesthesiologist. "Take her out."

Doctor Kevin would have protested but he could tell by her begging and the soft moans she released on her breaths that Doctor Tyler was right. He placed the scalpel on her chest so she could feel it as the gas took over.

Jade looked up at the lights then straight to Doctor Tyler as the mask came down over her face. Before she had felt fear or even a small sense of relief when she felt the soft black rubber press against her face. But this time, this time she felt unfulfilled. This time she hadn't felt his cock fill her. Jade did her best to fight the drug and keep her eyes open... Hoping he would change his mind, but her eyelids got heavier and heavier...as her eyes closed and she felt the cold scalpel rise with each deep breath, she thought she heard Doctor Tyler's voice whisper in her ear, "I'll be seeing you again very soon....."

<u>PART 10</u>

Doctor Tyler looked at Jade sleeping in her bed. Her blankets rising with each soft breath. She was still under the influence of the gas, but would wake up soon. He had followed the porters taking her back to her dorm, he was going to be there when she woke up.

Jade sighed in her sleep, her hand coming up to tuck her pillow into the nape of her soft neck, causing the blanket to slip lower on her chest. Doctor Tyler groaned low. Her collar bone now exposed, the small indentation at the base of her neck almost making a straight line for his eyes to go to her cleavage, but the blanket still hid it from view. Jade took a deeper breath as she moaned. Doctor Tyler could see the outline of her nipples poking up in the blanket. His hand moved down to the throbbing between his legs. He had planned on waiting for her to wake up and find him but one more soft moan and he wouldn't be able to wait.

Doctor Tyler started rubbing the bulge in his scrubs as he stared at her. Not that long ago she was naked and restrained to his surgical table at his mercy. Now the only thing that separated him from the view of her feminine body was the single satin sheet. He could just imagine the softness of the material brushing against her chest, barely able to keep from slipping off her breasts and down her stomach. Hmmmm oh how he wished she would roll or take a deep breath so it would. Jade took a breath almost the instant he thought it, causing his heart to stop and his cock to almost will the sheet lower. But instead of the sheet moving lower she moaned low and whispered in her sleep, "please doctor..."

Doctor Tyler let out a low groan, almost growl, he couldn't wait for her to wake up. Walking towards her bed he pulled off his scrub top, his eyes never leaving her face. He wasn't sure now if he wanted her to suddenly wake up or wanted her to stay dreaming so he could wake her. His fingers fumbled with the ties on his scrub pants before finally freeing them and letting them slide past his hips to the floor. He then nearly ripped off his underwear and placed one knee on her bed. The stain sheet silky against his naked body, but he knew it wouldn't compare to the softness if her skin.

Taking his knee off her bed he gently lifted the blanket and slipped underneath it, sliding closer to her body. He could feel her body heat as he got closer to her. Jades head turned towards him. Doctor Tyler took a breath and brought his hand up under the blanket to her chest. His fingertips lightly touching her skin, not wanting to wake her yet. Slowly placing his palm against her he moved it down between her breasts, bringing the sheet down with the movement of his hand. He moved lower, pausing just above her belly button to feel her take a breath and have her stomach arch up into his palm. Jade moaned again in her sleep,

Doctor Tyler bit his tongue and moved his hand lower. The heel of his hand finding the top of her pubic mound, about an inch from her clit.

Jade rolled onto her back, Doctor Tyler took the chance to slide his hand between her thighs and gently press against the inside of her right thigh. The small pressure caused her to move it in her sleep. Jade sighed. "Hmmmmm doctor...examine me." Doctor Tyler felt his cock jump. She was so wet. He was going to wake her up now, and he wanted to feel her body wake up with his cock deep inside of her.

Sitting up in her bed, Doctor Tyler put his hands together and between her legs, forcing them to spread a part and open up to him. Instantly he caught the scent of her arousal. She was excited, and dreaming of him. He moved between her legs, holding the tip of his cock against her slit.

Jades' body arched at the slight pressure against her entrance. Her eyes fluttered, she would be awake soon. Doctor Tyler pushed just the head of his cock inside of her. Her muscles wrapped around him, little waves of pleasure wanting more of him. The heat of her core so enticing he wanted to burry deep inside of her.

Bringing his hands up to her hips he pressed the palms against her body and slid them up her sides, over her stomach to her breasts. He cupped them in his hands squeezing them gently, watching her face as her lips parted and her eyes fluttered. He brushed his thumbs over her nipples, feeling them bud from the gentle touch. He then moved his hands up to her shoulders and leaned down a bit, whispering low, almost a command for his patient to obey doctors orders, "time to wake up Jade."

Jade moaned, her body felt a bit heavy, like her blankets had doubled. She moaned, "hmmmm Doctor Tyler." She dreamt of him standing at the foot of her bed, watching her, shaking his head at her excitement, ready to punish her. Her eyes shot open.

The moment Doctor Tyler saw Jades eyes open, he thrust his hips fast and hard, his cock filling her completely, forcing her body to take all of him. He leaned down and placed his lips against hers. He could feel her gasp and scream beneath his kiss, but that was the point. Her surprise made her vaginal core grip his shaft so tight he moaned against her. His cock pulsed, leaking pre cum. Her hands came up and grabbed his back. They moved fast at first then he felt her palms press against his body, and slowly rub up and down, as though not believing he was real.

Doctor Tyler placed his hands on the pillow beside her head. He could feel her nipples against his chest as she started to pant. Her wetness continuing to grow as he started to pump his hips, his cock sliding in and out slowly, filling her. Her hips bucking with each thrust, brining her clit up to brush against his body.

Doctor Tyler moved his lips and kissed her

neck, listening to her pant for air as he gently nipped her neck. She moaned low. Doctor Tyler whispered, "cum for me now young lady."

Jade took a quick breath and groaned. "Yessssss Doctor." She could not only feel each thrust of his hips but hear them as well, she was so wet, so excited. Her vaginal core finally feeling filled. Feeling him inside of her as she woke up. Her muscles gripped him tight as pleasure shot from her clit, the dominance of him holding her down and claiming her adding to her arousal.

Doctor Tyler felt her body shake under his, her hips coming up to his as her muscles surrounded his cock and milked him in wave after wave of pleasure, causing him to cum at the same time. He moaned against her as she screamed for him.

Doctor Tyler felt his cock explode inside of her, filling her, claiming her as his. His heart pounding, feeling her body grip him in small waves of aftershock pleasure. He closed his eyes just to feel her body gripping him, holding him inside of her. As her body slowly relaxed under his, he kissed her lips again. "Remember young lady." He kissed her lips, "you are mine." He bit her neck a bit harder, feeling her muscles grip his cock tight as he did, making him moan. "Mine to punish..." He looked back up at her, her eyes coming into contact and lost in his. He grinned and thrust his hips, making his cock slide just a bit deeper and brush her cervix. Jade let out a little scream of pleasure and he felt her wetness trickle out and over his balls. "Mine to give pleasure."

    Jade pressed her hands against his back, her fingernails gripping him as though holding him tight against her body just so she could feel him. Her muscles still holding onto his shaft. She couldn't look away from his eyes if she tried. As much as she might struggle or try to get off his surgical table, he was right. She was at his mercy. She was his. "Yes Doctor."

The Visiting Surgeon Book 5: Part 1

<u>The Visiting Surgeon 5</u>

<u>PART 1</u>

Jade took a deep breath as she tied the surgical mask against her face. She stared at the wall in front of her. It was nothing special. Just a wall with a shelf containing different sized masks, disposal scrub caps and scrub brushes. Her eyes drifted down to the steel sink as she took a scrub brush and started scrubbing up. As the pink solution foamed over her hands she thought of him...her surgeon.

The way the mask hid his plans while his eyes peered over it, down at her. Full of dominance and control. Full of skill and sexual desire. Oh sure he tried to hide it, but whenever she turned her head on his table, she could catch the bulge growing in his, and the other doctors, scrubs. His hands also changed as they touched her. Though he would still be clinical in the way he explored her abdomen or spread her lips to expose her clit, his fingers moved faster. The more he got excited he would touch her pussy and feel the silky wetness covering his gloved fingers. Sometimes he would press just a little firmer against her clit to make her more excited. But other times he would go just a bit softer, making her hips buck for more. More of his touch. More of him.

"You know, if you scrub away all of your skin, you won't be able to do the surgery."

Jade jumped as the voice cut into her thoughts. Her stomach tightened and a little wetness tickled out onto her panties as her mind remembered how the surgeon caught her masturbating last time. She swallowed and turned around. Letting out a breath, she wasn't sure if she was happy or disappointed to find Ann standing behind her. "Guess I'm just nervous."

"Don't blame you. Just glad you were picked first to do the operation and not me!!"

Jade ran her forearms under the water bringing the stream down from her elbows to her fingers washing away the pink foam. "Ya, but at least Doctor Peters is pretty forgiving on newbs." She winked at her friend as she backed up against the operating room doors.

"Didn't you hear? Doctor Peters switched out. There's a new surgeon that's going to be watching you."

Jade stopped dead in the doorway, swearing her heart did the same. She had studied her ass off for the procedure and knew she could do it, but had been nervous the moment her name came up. Her saving grace, during studying, had been knowing Doctor Peters would be watching her, one of the only teachers she felt at ease with. Also one of the doctors she was sure hadn't seen her naked strapped to the visiting surgeons table...or if he had he hadn't given any signs that he had. "No."

Ann smiled as Jade looked like a deer in the headlights. "Don't know who it is but, good luck!!

I'll be with the others watching from the observation room."

"Thanks." Jade thought it sounded sarcastic as Ann turned around and headed off, but she couldn't help it. Taking a breath she walked into the operating room, turning around to face a couple nurses. One of them came up to her as she unfolded the sterile gloves on the small rolling table and then the gown and put it on, the nurse tying it behind her. Jade then put on the gloves, snapping one on and then the other over the cuffs of the gown. Taking a breath and trying to hide it behind her mask, she turned back to the table. The anesthesiologist smiled, a genuine one that reached his eyes, and her heart skipped a beat. Could he have been the one at her head? The one that brought the soft black rubber mask over her nose and mouth? Forcing her into submission, or giving her sweet oxygen to recover after a hard orgasm?

Hmmmm, she moaned inside her head. That was something she sure could use right now. Her heart was pounding so hard in her chest she thought she was going to pass out from nerves. Her eyes quickly moved to the nurse at the table, already gowned and waiting. The patient was on the table and partly covered. Jade wiggled her nose and felt the mask move across her cheeks and lips. She wondered if that was something the surgeon felt when he stared down at her.

Did he know the power he held just by wearing it? How her stomach tightened and her clit tingled?

How her excitement made her start to get wet just by looking at him? Did he feel the mask against his face as he sat between her legs? And if he did, did he wish he wasn't wearing it so he could lick her puffy labia or suck her clit? Or did having to wear it for years of practice make it unnoticeable for him?

Jade stepped up to the table and took the sterile sheets from the nurse. The two of them opened them up over the patient, leaving only the small part of the abdomen open for the operation. The sheets effectively hiding the patient. It made it a bit easier, and the beeps of the heart monitor blurred into the back ground. Jade reached up and put the sterile covers over the surgical lights' middle handle and tilted them into a better position. It was about the only thing she was allowed to do without her supervising surgeon in the room watching her.

Her vaginal muscles contracted as she thought of the surgeon watching her, of all the doctors watching her. Watching her nipples bud, the small goose bumps on her skin form from the cool air of the operating room and excitement. Watching as her hips bucked against the restraints and her wetness grew giving away her excitement.

"Nervous?"

The male voice sent a shiver down her spine and made her physically jump in surprise. "Yes doctor."

The surgeon nodded to the nurse across from Jade who started setting out the skin knife and a couple other instruments. He got closer to her and whispered, "let's hope it's just nerves and not loosing focus. Otherwise you'll be saying 'yes doctor' for a whole other reason."

Jade felt her stomach turn and her clit tingle. The voice was familiar but because he had spoken so low to make sure the others in the operating room didn't hear, it had made it hard to place. But one thing was for certain, whomever was supervising her had definitely watched her struggle, beg, and cum, on the surgeons table. And she guessed, had switched with Doctor Peters on purpose.

BONUS STORY

THE MASK

<u>THE MASK</u>

Her fever was high, she could feel it, especially when she looked at things. The edges seemed blurred, like in movies when they did flash backs, though it seemed more like she was dreaming really. But what had really tipped her off was someone telling her that she had a fever and it was high. It was one of two things that had actually stuck with her, that and hearing the word surgery. Oh gawd! that was all she needed. A hot doctor, all scrubbed up, and hiding behind that mask. Ok, so it was necessary for their work, but damn it...it made them hot. It gave her butterflies just thinking about it...and those butterflies...well let's just say she was pretty sure she couldn't blame all of her bodily reactions on her fever.

She could just picture it now, being wheeled down the hallway, looking at the fluorescent lights in the ceiling. Knowing she wouldn't be able to avoid it, she would soon be in the hands of a hot skilled doctor, surgeon at that. Who would see every inch of her body. There would be no hiding anything, and definitely not being able to hide her embarrassment. Could imagine herself being put on something cold and feeling hands over shoulders. Running lower, gently following the curve of her breasts, maybe staying on them for just a moment longer, cupping them between his fingers, quickly as though he didn't want anyone noticing his actions, before moving lower. Feeling over her abdomen and down her legs. She groaned softly at the touch. Not that it really hurt, oh no, more so that it was gentle, yet commanding. As if it were not only assessing her body, but memorizing every inch to take command of it.

There was movement and then she would feel the cold blade of the scissors...yes the scissors, her clothes were being cut from her body. Exposing her soft creamy skin to his eyes, his hands, his mercy. She tried to move to fight it, but she was in such a daze, or she would be. Giving up to the doctor, her surgeon, she laid there, exposing her body.

Maybe he would tell the staff to leave for a moment, hmm yes, she could hear the doors now and the questioning murmurs of the people as they left the room. Naked and alone in the operating room with the doctor. He would walk around her, his latex covered fingers gently touching her body and sliding down her skin as he walked around the table, giving time for his coworkers to be out of viewing range and ear shot. She blinked her eyes for a second, feeling tired, opening them she stared directly into the eyes of the surgeon looking down on her. Oh the shivers that ran down her body. It was like staring into complete power and control, while having none of it herself. All the while knowing she was naked and exposed to his every whim and mercy. His hand would slide down her neck, teasing her as he took her pulse. Oh gawd, she could never hide anything from her doctor. Surely he could feel her pulse racing, now, beneath his fingertips. His fingers then continued down to her chest. His voice was low, she couldn't make out the words, but she imagined him telling her to be a good patient, to listen and to trust her doctor. Maybe he would even order her not to move, like that would be easy with the way his hand was commanding her breasts. Grabbing them so the nipple was in his palm, his fingers moving down her breast to her chest and then pulling up, as though milking and massaging them. She groaned. Her moaning causing him to pull his hand all the way up, extending and stretching her nipples. Though it wouldn't hurt, she knew it would send shots of electric pleasure throughout her body, and make her nipples rock hard. Budding for his pleasure, after all, it would be his exam that caused them to get so excited.

She rolled her head to the side, closing her eyes for a moment, taking a breath. She could imagine his hand moving to her abdomen, slowly palpating across each quarter. His finger tips digging slightly into her body and moving in soft circles. She wasn't sure why she imagined herself squirming in certain locations, but figured it was her fever dream, so the fever must have given her some oddity in the dream. Hell, next she knew, her hot surgeon could turn into a pink elephant, or even Freddie Kruger! She shuddered at the thought and focused in on feeling the fingertips against her skin. There was a strange tapping sensation. Part of her loved the motion, the smooth rhythmic tap, while, at some points, it almost caused her that same strange pain sensation. Gawd she could just see Freddie showing up now, with his long fingernail type claws becoming the sharp cold steel of the surgeon's scalpel. No, she had to focus on the hot doctor image. She blinked and looked towards where the feeling of the gloved hand was coming from. The blurred edges messing with her perception a bit, but she could still make out the hot body under the tight scrubs.

It was obvious her surgeon worked out. The scrubs formed his ass perfectly, and his scrub top left her wanting to climb up off his table and strip it from his body, giving him her own personal exam. She moaned her approval and saw the figure turn his head to look at her. There was that dammed mask again. Blocking everything but his eyes. It was a mix between the hidden captor and the hot male predator beneath it. Oh she wanted his hands on her...everywhere...and she thought they were.

Moving lower, his hands touched her thighs and pushed, spreading them open. She closed her eyes and took a breath. She should fight him, make it at least a bit difficult for him, but she couldn't...and part of her didn't want too, wanted him to be in control of her. His fingers moving between her legs. She could feel him spreading her lips, exposing her further and looking for her clit....and he found it. Could feel his fingers touch and pull back on her clitoral hood, his finger coming up and lightly stroking the exposed bud. She gasped and once again saw the figure look at her. She swore if she could look beneath that mask he would be grinning the smile of a chestier cat. But her assessment of his body language could never prepare her for what happened next.

Keeping a thumb rubbing her clit, two fingers expertly slipped into her entrance. She gasped, moaning as she arched back into the operating table. Did she just hear male laughter mocking her? Oh she would like to smack that mask right of his face...but right now...oh right now...hmmmm....his thumb teased her clit...what was she thinking about again? Gawd her mind was so foggy. His fingers danced inside of her, she moaned, her hips starting to buck of their own accord, but he never missed a beat. His thumb rubbing her clit, his fingers almost waving inside of her. Curling back towards her entrance before thrusting out straight inside of her again. Her breathing quickened. Pressing his thumb against her clit, he rotated his palm so his fingertips now pressed up inside of her. His thumb went back to rotating against her clit sending waves of pleasure through her lower abdomen, but he wasn't finished yet.

His fingers stroked lightly against her, as if feeling for something in his internal exam...and he found it. The moment his smooth gloved fingers hit her G-spot intense pleasure shot throughout her body. She felt herself shake as she was filled with pleasure. His other hand moved to her lower abdomen and rubbed back and forth slowly, in time with the fingers inside of her. He pressed in on her clit and stroked her G-spot, and before she knew it she shook hard, and could swear she screamed with pleasure as she came all over his hand and his operating table. Resting his hand on her stomach, feeling her breathe each time she took an excited breath. He slowly withdrew his finger inside of her and pulled his hand up and over her clit. Even as she slipped between dazed pleasure and foggy fever dream, she could feel his fingers stroking her inside as he left her warm wet sheath.

She thought she heard a male voice telling her she was a good patient, listening to doctors orders, but that was crazy...and certainly something Freddie Kruger would never say. Gloved hands touched her thighs again, bringing them together. This was certainly a strange but amazing dream...after her fever breaks she was going to hope to constantly get fevers! She groaned her disapproval at hiding her pussy once again, wanting his personal exam to continue on.

Noises came from somewhere in the distance and she tried to find the hot surgeon. But she couldn't. She thought maybe it was the foggy edges keeping her from seeing him, so she tried sitting up. Dizziness instantly hit her, but she still tried. Her eyes moved as quick as they would let her before she laid back down. Licking her lips she closed her eyes and heard the voices getting closer. Opening her eyes, at the sounds of voices, she looked right into the eyes of the surgeon. The mask getting tighter on his face as she stared at him, as though someone was tying it right then. She saw his hands up, gloved, as he leaned in closer to her. She could see his mouth was moving, as his mask was moving. She focused hard, the blurred edges framing the eerie, yet incredibly hot mask, and his eyes.

"Are you ready?"

Wow, she understood that. All she could do was nod, hoping that it meant his fingers would take control of her body again, but as she looked up she saw a black rubber mask moving towards her face. Her heart raced as it came down and covered her mouth and nose. It wasn't long before she felt herself slipping away into dream land...but wait...if she was only now going to sleep....had before really been a fever dream as she thought?...or was this how they normally prepped a patient for surgery?

Her eyes blinked as she took a breath, and the surgeon once again moved into her field of vision. Another slow deep breath, she looked at him, wanting to ask so many questions...Her eyes closed for a moment then opened as she thought about the pleasure that had pooled in her lower abdomen and shot throughout her body. She looked right at that masked face, the man behind it in complete and total control...he winked at her and she gasped, taking in that last breath that took her into dreamland.

All characters and stories are fictional.

When practicing Medical Fetish, or any BDSM, be safe, have consent, and have fun.

Lyric loves to hear from her readers.

medicalfetishwriter@gmail.com